4/15

D1252800

Perfectly
POPPY

The Big Bike

Story by Michele Jakubowski

Pictures by Erica-Jane Waters

Picture Window Books

Perfectly Poppy is published by Picture Window Books, a Capstone Imprint
1710 Roe Crest Drive, North Mankato, MN 56003
www.capstonepub.com

Library of Congress Cataloging-in-Publication Data
Jakubowski, Michele, author.
The big bike / by Michele Jakubowski ; illustrated by Erica-Jane Waters.
pages cm. -- (Perfectly Poppy) z
Summary: Poppy is excited about getting a big-girl bike, but when she sees the bike she
becomes apprehensive about actually riding it.
ISBN 978-1-4795-5801-8 (hardcover) -- ISBN 978-1-4795-5805-6 (pbk.)
ISBN 978-1-4795-6203-9 (ebook pdf)
1. Bicycles--Juvenile fiction. 2. Self-confidence--Juvenile fiction. [1. Bicycles and bicycling--
Fiction. 2. Self-confidence--Fiction.] I. Waters, Erica-Jane, illustrator. II. Title.
PZ7.J153555Bg 2015
813.6--dc23   2014013455

Image credits: Shutterstock
Designer: Kristi Carlson

Printed in China by Nordica
0914/CA21401511
092014   00847ONORDS15

Table of Contents

Chapter 1

A New Bike

It was a big day for Poppy.

She was getting a new bike!

Poppy had worked very hard to

learn how to ride her old bike,

but it was too small now.

"I'm going to miss my old bike," Poppy told her best friend, Millie. "But my new bike will have a basket and a bell."

"That sounds really cool," Millie said.

"My dad is bringing it home after work," Poppy said.

"You are so lucky," Millie said.

"My mom and dad said we could take a bike ride together this weekend," Poppy said.

"Where would we go?" Millie asked.

"They said we could take the trail that leads all the way to the park!" Poppy said.

"We never get to go that far!" Millie said.

"I know! It is a long ride, so my mom said she'll pack us a picnic," Poppy said.

"You love food!" Millie said.

"And you love the park," Poppy said. "Now I just need my new bike."

Chapter 2

A Very Big Bike

After Millie left, Poppy couldn't
wait for her dad to come home
with her new bike. Finally, she saw
his car pull into the driveway.

"My new bike is here!" she

shouted as she ran out the door.

Poppy's mom and older

brother, Nolan, followed her

outside. They got there just as

Poppy's dad took her new bike

out of the car.

"Wow!" her mom said.

"That's awesome!" Nolan said.

He never thought anything of

Poppy's was awesome.

But Poppy just stood there

with her mouth open.

Finally she said, "It's so big."

"It is big," her dad said. He brought the bike over to Poppy. "But you're a big kid now, so you need a big bike."

Poppy looked at her old bike.

It was small and easy to ride. This

new bike looked scary.

"Get on, Poppy," her dad said.

"No, thank you," she said.

"Come on, Poppy," her mom said. "Don't be scared."

"I'm not scared," said Poppy.

"I just like my old bike better."

"Really?" her dad asked.

"Really," Poppy told him.
"You can take this one back to
the store."

"You don't even want to try
it?" her dad asked.

"Not really," Poppy said.

Poppy's mom put her arm around her shoulder.

"Don't worry, Poppy," she said. "You'll get used to this bike in no time."

Poppy wasn't so sure, but she did agree to keep the bike.

Chapter 3

The Best Bike

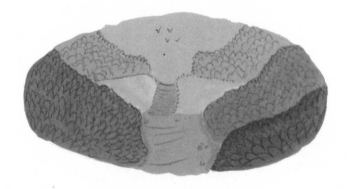

By Saturday, Poppy was still unsure about her new bike. She had ridden it on the driveway a few times. She hadn't fallen, but she was still scared.

The trail was long. She wasn't sure she could make it all the way to the park on her big bike.

Millie quickly
put on her elbow
pads, kneepads,
and helmet. Poppy
put on her gear
very slowly.

"Let's go!" Millie said.

She hopped on her bike and
raced away. Nolan and his friend
Thomas raced by, too.

"Come on, Poppy!" Nolan said.
"We don't have all day."

"Just a minute," Poppy said.

She watched as Nolan, Thomas, and Millie sped down the trail without her. She didn't like being left behind.

Poppy took a deep breath and started pedaling. At first, she was shaky. Then she pedaled a little faster and felt better.

The faster she went, the more
confident she felt. By the time
they got to the park, Poppy felt
great. She loved her new bike!

"I can ride so much faster on my new bike," Poppy told Millie.

"Do you still miss your old bike?" Millie asked.

"Not at all!" Poppy said with a smile. "This bike is the best!"

Poppy's New Words

I learned so many new words today! I made sure to write them down so I could use them again.

confident (KON-fuh-duhnt) — believing in yourself and abilities

elbow pads (EL-boh PADZ) — protective pads worns over your elbows

gear (GIHR) — equipment or clothing

helmet (HEL-mit) — a hard hat that protects your head

kneepads (NEE-padz) — protective pads worn over your knees

unsure (uhn-SHOOR) — not certain

Poppy's Ponders

After our long bike ride, I had some time to think. Here are some of my questions and thoughts from the day.

1. Biking is my favorite activity. What is your favorite activity? Why?

2. Even though I like my new bike, I'm still sad to lose my old one. Talk about something you are sad to lose now that you are bigger.

3. I was really scared to try my new bike. Write about a time when you were scared.

4. If you could have any bike in the world, what would it look like? Draw a picture to match your description.

Bike Fun and Games

I love biking around my neighborhood, but I also love to play these bike games with Millie.

Bike Challenge

Draw a wide chalk line down your driveway or sidewalk. You can make it straight, curvy, or a figure-eight shape. You can even make a few different courses if you would like. Take turns timing each other on the courses. See how fast and how slow you can go without stopping.

Bike Wash

Instead of a car wash, have a bike wash! Grab a hose, a bucket, soap, a sponge, and a towel and get scrubbing. You might even earn some money!

Bike Horse

Pretend your bike is a horse. Give your horse a name, make a stall, and be sure to ride and take care of it. Be creative and have fun!

Obstacle Course

Using buckets, cones, jump ropes, and other items from your garage, create an obstacle course. See who can go the fastest and who can go the slowest without stopping.

About the Author

Raised in the Chicago suburb of Hoffman Estates, Michele Jakubowski has the teachers in her life to thank for her love of reading and writing. While writing has always been a passion for Michele, she believes it is the books she has read throughout the years, and the teachers who assigned them, that have made her the storyteller she is today. Michele lives in Powell, Ohio, with her husband, John, and their children, Jack and Mia.

About the Illustrator

Erica-Jane Waters grew up in the beautiful Northern Irish countryside, where her imagination was ignited by the local folklore and fairytales. She now lives in Oxfordshire, England, with her young family. Erica writes and illustrates children's books and creates art for magazines, greeting cards, and various other projects.